THIS BOOK
BELONGS TO

JAYSON

With love!
Kisses

Narine
x x x x

SBN 361 00419 2

Published by Purnell Books, Paulton, Bristol,
BS18 5LQ, a member of the BPCC group of companies.
Reprinted 1983
Made and printed in Great Britain by Purnell and Sons
(Book Production) Ltd, Paulton, Bristol.

# NODDY

## HAS AN ADVENTURE

### BY
### Enid Blyton

## CONTENTS

**LONDON**
**SAMPSON LOW, MARSTON & CO. LTD.**
**AND DENNIS DOBSON LTD.**

© Enid Blyton
as to the text herein and
Sampson Low, Marston & Co. Ltd.
as to the artwork herein 1958

"MILKO!" CALLED THE MILKMAN AT THE TOP
OF HIS VOICE

6

## 1. A VISIT FROM BIG-EARS

"OH what a long day I've had!" said little Noddy, finishing his supper. "I'm too tired to wash up the dirty dishes. I'll do them tomorrow morning."

He got up, yawning a very big yawn, and looked at his little bed.

"I feel so sleepy
And yawny and dozy
And you, little bed,
Look so lovely and cosy!
I'll soon be cuddled
Beneath your sheet,
And fast asleep
From my head to my feet!"

He cleaned his teeth and brushed his hair.

He undressed and washed himself very well indeed. Then he sat down to take off his red shoes. He leaned back in his chair for a minute, and yawned again. And dear me, he fell fast asleep. His head nodded and his bell rang and jingled.

The jingling woke him up, and he opened his eyes and looked round. "What's that noise? Who's ringing a bell? Is it someone at the front door at this time of night?"

He got up and went to the door. No, there was no one there. "How silly I am—it was the bell on my hat, ringing when my head nodded and I fell asleep!" said Noddy.

He blew out his candle and jumped into his little bed. He snuggled down cosily.

"It's dark and it's quiet,
I'm going to sleep;
My eyes are tight shut,
They can't even peep;
I'll dream of old Big-Ears,
And dear Tessie Bear;

8

## A VISIT FROM BIG-EARS

I'm going to Dreamland,
And now——

I——

   am——

     THERE!"
And so he was, fast
asleep, dreaming of

having tea with Big-Ears and little Tessie Bear.

Noddy was very, very tired after his long and busy day, and he didn't wake up even when the milkman came and popped his bottle of milk down on the door-step.

"Milko!" called the milkman, wondering if little Noddy would come to the door and let him tap his head to make it nod, as he usually did. The milkman did so love doing that. But this morning no Noddy appeared.

"Fast asleep, I suppose," said the milkman and went on his way, shouting "Milko" at the top of his voice.

Someone else came to Noddy's house soon after that. Someone riding fast on a bicycle. It was Big-Ears, and he didn't look very pleased. He jumped off his bicycle, stood it against the wall of Noddy's little house, and banged at the door.

"NODDY!" he called, "ARE YOU IN?"

Noddy woke up with a start, and sat up in bed. "Oh Big-Ears! You woke me up with such a jump!" he said. "What's the matter? Come in!"

Big-Ears opened the door and walked in. He looked so cross that Noddy stared at him in surprise.

"What's wrong, Big-Ears?" he said.

"Noddy, I want you to tell me something," said Big-Ears, sitting down in the chair. "Did

you play a trick on me last night?"

"Last night? No, of course not," said Noddy, in wonder. "I was so tired that I went to bed quite early, and I fell asleep at once—and I've only just woken up. Whatever do you mean?"

"NODDY," SAID BIG-EARS, "I WANT YOU TO TELL
ME SOMETHING"

11

"Well—I woke up last night, and heard a car coming slowly up the woodland path to my front gate," said Big-Ears. "And it stopped there. I thought perhaps it was you, come to see me very late."

"Well, it wasn't," said Noddy. "And it

wasn't *my* car either. That was fast asleep in its little garage. What happened? Did the car go away?"

"It stayed for a little while," said Big-Ears. "Then it suddenly said 'parp-parp!' in exactly the same voice as yours does—and drove off!"

"Well, I don't see why you should come banging at my door and waking me up with a jump, just because someone stopped his car outside your house last night, Big-Ears," said Noddy. "You look so cross about it too!"

"Yes, but wait a bit," said Big-Ears. "When

I went out into my garden this morning, I found that all the washing I'd left hanging out last night had been unpegged and taken away! Are you *sure* you didn't play a silly trick on me last night, Noddy?"

"NO," said Noddy, his head nodding up and down angrily, for all the world as if he were saying "YES". "I did NOT play a trick on you. And please go away, Big-Ears, if you're going to look as cross as that. I'm going to get dressed."

So Big-Ears got up, and went off without another word. Noddy ran to the window to watch him get on his bicycle and ride away.

"Well!" said Noddy. "He doesn't believe me! As if I'd do a silly thing like that! Now I'd better hurry up and get my car and go out, or I'll never make any money today."

## 2. NODDY HAS ANOTHER BUSY DAY

NODDY had a very busy day. He took the clock-work mouse to the market to do his shopping.
, "Clickity-click, I must be quick," said the little mouse. "Oh, you're sitting on my tail, Noddy."

"What a nuisance tails are!" said Noddy, pushing the mouse's tail away. "I'm glad *I* haven't one. I'd cut it off if I had."

"Oooh, you wouldn't!" said the mouse, shocked.

"Have you heard my song about tails?" said Noddy, thinking of one at that very moment.

"No. And I don't want to hear it if it's a rude one," said the mouse. "Nor does my tail."

"It isn't rude. It's just funny, like your tail," said Noddy, and he began to sing.

"Oh tails are a nuisance,
And shouldn't be grown,
How thankful I am
That I've none of my own.
Tails, tails, tails!
Tails that wag,
Tails that drag,
Tails that wriggle and shake,
Tails that quiver,
Tails that shiver,
And tails that curl like a snake!
Oh tails are a nuisance,
And . . ."

"I think that's enough," said the clockwork mouse. "It's a silly song, not a funny one. Here's the market, Noddy. Let me get down. I've a good mind to charge you sixpence for making me listen to such a silly song."

Away he went, his long thin tail wriggling behind him, looking rather offended. Noddy laughed. "Oh dear—the clockwork mouse is very touchy.

Hallo, here's someone else who wants to hire my car. Good morning, Mrs. Noah. How are all the animals?"

"They're all well and happy, except one of the elephants," said Mrs. Noah, getting into the car. "He's quarrelled with the lions, and he wants to leave the ark. He keeps saying he will pack his trunk and go."

Noddy laughed and laughed, and almost knocked a lamp-post over. "I must remember to tell that joke to old Big-Ears," he said. And then he remembered that Big-Ears hadn't been very nice to him. Oh dear — poor Big-Ears. Had he got his washing back yet?

He took Mrs. Noah back to the ark, and then he went to the station to meet the train. There was usually someone who wanted to hire his car when the train came in.

"Chuffity-chuffity-huffity-puffity!" The little toy train drew in at the platform, and plenty of

NODDY RAN TO COLLECT KATIE KITTEN'S LUGGAGE

17

passengers jumped out. One waved her umbrella at Noddy, and he ran to collect her luggage.

It was Katie Kitten, back from a visit to her Auntie Furry. She jumped into the car, and Noddy put her bag at the back. Off they went.

"Any news since I've been away?" asked Katie Kitten.

"Not much," said Noddy, "except that Micky Monkey climbed a tree to steal some apples, and tied his tail to a branch so that he wouldn't fall —and he couldn't untie the knot when he wanted to climb down again!"

"Oh—was he caught then?" said Katie, in delight. "He's always up to mischief."

"Yes. The farmer caught him," said Noddy. "Oh and another piece of news is that someone took all Big-Ears' washing off the line last night— someone in a car. He thought I'd played him a trick—but I wouldn't do a thing like that."

"No, of course not. I wonder who *did* take it, though," said Katie Kitten. "Here's my house,

Noddy. And here's sixpence for my fare. Good-bye!"

And out she got, and went into her little house with her bag. Noddy turned his car round and wondered if he should go and call on old Big-Ears. Perhaps he wouldn't be so cross now.

So off he went, parp-parp, up to Big-Ears' toadstool house in the woods. He jumped out at the gate and went to the door and knocked. Then he saw a notice on the door.

### GONE OUT. BACK TONIGHT.

"Oh bother!" said Noddy. "I *wonder* who came last night and took Big-Ears' washing. I'll look and see if there are any tyre marks outside the gate."

So he went to look, but he couldn't see any. The ground was much too hard and dry.

"Well—I'm going home," said Noddy, and got back into his car. "I've done a lot today and I'm tired and hungry. Oh dear—what a pity Big-Ears is out. I could have had tea with him and a nice rest. Wherever can he have gone? Perhaps he is looking for his washing!"

Away went Noddy to House-for-One, his bell jingling merrily. Now for a nice supper—then he would do his new jig-saw—and then he would snuggle down into bed.

"And you can snuggle down in your garage, little car," said Noddy.

"Parp-parp," said the car, happily, and raced down the road at top speed. "Parp-parp!"

## 3. A VISIT FROM MR. PLOD

NEXT morning, just as Noddy was busily washing his car, he saw Mr. Plod the policeman coming along on his bicycle. Noddy waved his duster at him.

"Hallo, Mr. Plod! Have you caught many robbers lately?"

"No. But I'm after one now," said Mr. Plod, and jumped off his bicycle.

"Oooh, are you—how exciting!" said Noddy. "Who's the thief? What has he stolen?"

"He went to Mr. Big-Bear's garden last night and picked all his flowers," said Mr. Plod. "Yes, every single one! I suppose he means to sell them."

"Did Mr. Big-Bear see the thief?" asked Noddy. "Why—he might have been the same fellow who stole Big-Ears' washing, Mr. Plod!"

"He probably *was*," said Mr. Plod. "He came in a car, Noddy, just as he did at Big-Ears' the night before!"

"Well, don't you dare to say it was *my* car, Mr. Plod!" said Noddy, fiercely. "Because it wasn't! I was in bed, and my car was in its garage."

"Mr. Big-Bear said he heard it give a very quiet parp-parp in your car's voice," said Mr. Plod. "Everyone knows the sound of your car's hooter, Noddy. Are you quite sure you're not playing tricks?"

Noddy was so cross that he actually stamped his foot at Mr. Plod. The car was angry too and began to sound its hooter very loudly indeed. "PARP PARP PARP PARP PARP."

"Now you be quiet," said Mr. Plod to the car. "What with Noddy stamping around and you parping at me like that, I shall begin to lose my temper. Noddy, did you..."

"I didn't, didn't, didn't," said Noddy, not waiting for Mr. Plod to finish his question.

"Noddy, will you please be quiet and let me ask you some qu..." began Mr. Plod again.

"I won't, won't, won't," cried Noddy.

Mr. Plod took out his notebook and pencil. "Noddy, I must ask you if you were out last night," he said.

"I wasn't, wasn't, wasn't!" said Noddy and stamped his foot.

"PARP PARP PARP!" said the car at the top of its voice.

"No more wasn'ts and won'ts and didn'ts, please," said Mr. Plod sternly. "And no more parps from *you*, car, either."

And then someone suddenly ran joyfully up and jumped lovingly at Noddy. He sat down with a bump.

"Oh Bumpy-Dog—it's you!" he said. "Look—go and jump up at Mr. Plod, not me!"

The Bumpy-Dog rushed at the surprised Mr. Plod at once and leapt up at him, his tongue hanging out in excitement. Mr. Plod sat down suddenly, too, and the Bumpy-Dog licked his face all over, and wouldn't let him get up.

"DON'T!" roared Mr. Plod at Bumpy. But Bumpy never seemed to know what "Don't" meant, and every time the policeman tried to get up, Bumpy leapt at him and made him sit down with a bump again.

"I'll lock you up, you pest of a dog!" shouted Mr. Plod. "Noddy, call him off!"

"Bumpy—come here," said Noddy, and Bumpy left Mr. Plod and ran at once to Noddy, who fell over again as Bumpy sprang at him lovingly. Noddy put his arms round Bumpy's neck and whispered to him.

"Chase Mr. Plod away, Bumpy, please!"

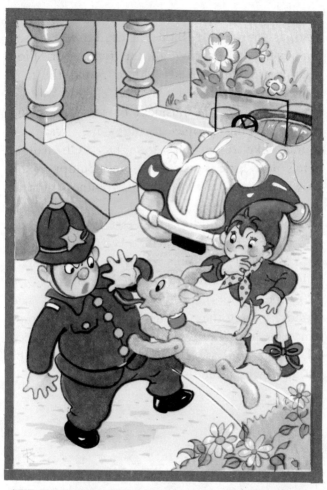

THE BUMPY-DOG RUSHED AT MR. PLOD AND LEAPT
UP AT HIM

So, as soon as Mr. Plod got up, Bumpy chased him excitedly, barking all the time. Mr. Plod disappeared very quickly indeed round the next corner. Noddy heaved a sigh of relief.

"I don't like this business of someone going round robbing people at night in a car that sounds like mine," he thought. "Oh hallo— here's dear little Tessie Bear—and Bumpy again. Down, Bumpy, down! Oh my goodness, what a dog!"

"Hallo, little Noddy," said Tessie Bear. "Bumpy and I have come to see you. What's the matter with Mr. Plod? He came round the corner at sixty miles an hour and nearly knocked me over."

"Come indoors and I'll tell you, Tessie," said Noddy, giving her a hug. "We'll have some lemonade and a bun. No, *not* you, Bumpy. Keep off, I tell you! Good gracious, I seem to be sitting down all the time you're with me!"

## 4. TESSIE HAS A PLAN

NODDY and Tessie Bear were soon enjoying lemonade and buns. Bumpy sat in a third chair, wagging his tail all the time. Thumpity-thumpity-thump it went against the back of the chair.

Noddy told Tessie Bear about Big-Ears and his stolen washing, and about Mr. Big-Bear's flowers.

"All picked and taken away!" said Noddy. "And Mr. Big-Bear heard a car saying 'parp-parp' like mine does, but very, very quietly. And they *both* think it might be me playing tricks! Playing tricks! Good gracious, those aren't tricks, they're stealing."

"Oh dear," said Tessie Bear, nibbling her bun. "You'll have to do something about it, Noddy, before people begin to think it must be you. Everybody knows the parp-parp noise your car makes. It isn't a bit like anyone else's car. Do you suppose anybody is borrowing your hooter?"

"Good gracious, no!" said Noddy. "I would miss it if they did. It's always on my car each morning. Besides my garage is locked when the car is there. Bumpy, stop licking the sugar off those buns!"

"Wuff, wuff," said Bumpy, and jumped down from his chair. He tried to get on to Noddy's knee.

"Oh do get down," said Noddy. "Tessie, did you ever know such a licky dog? I shall really have to get a towel to wipe off his licks. My hanky is too small. Down, Bumpy, down!"

"Bumpy!" said Tessie in a stern little voice

that Noddy had never heard before. To his surprise Bumpy stopped prancing about, lay down, put his head on his paws, and stayed quite still.

"However do you make him do that, Tessie?" said Noddy, astonished. "What a wonderful thing! You really are clever. Have another bun? Or would you like a biscuit?"

At the word "biscuit" Bumpy shot to his feet again, and leapt on Noddy with a glad woof.

"Oh *don't*!" said Noddy. "Just as I was praising you, too. For goodness' sake go out into the garden, Bumpy."

He shooed Bumpy into the garden and shut the door. Bumpy immediately put his head in at the window, with his two front paws.

"All right. Stay there and listen to everything," said Noddy. "But DON'T come in."

"Noddy," said Tessie Bear, "do you suppose anyone is borrowing your *car* at night—getting into your garage, and running it out—and then putting it back again?"

"Oh no, Tessie," said Noddy. "I told you my

29

garage was *locked* each night. And, anyway, if anyone tried to take my car it would hoot and hoot and hoot, and wake me up."

"Yes, of course," said Tessie. "Well, look, Noddy, you come and stay with me tonight, and then if anything is stolen, and anyone hears a parp-parp noise, we can PROVE it isn't you."

"Oh Tessie—that *is* a good idea," said Noddy, pleased. "But wait! I don't really like leaving my little house empty—because if there *is* a robber about, he might come and steal all *my* things!"

"Well, why not leave Bumpy here to guard everything," said Tessie. She turned to Bumpy, who was still listening at the window. "You'd

like to guard Noddy's house, wouldn't you, Bumpy-Dog?"

Bumpy was so over-joyed at being spoken to again that he leapt in at the window and rushed to lick Tessie. "Wuff!" he said happily. "Wuff-wuff-WUFF!"

NODDY FLAPPED BUMPY AWAY WITH A CUSHION

31

Then he tried to lick Noddy, but Noddy was ready for him and flapped him away with a cushion.

"Yes, Tessie, that's a good idea," said Noddy. "I *will* come and spend the night at your house, and we'll certainly leave Bumpy here. I'll leave my car here too, because you haven't a garage. Now I'd better get the car out and go and do some work. Would you like to come with me?"

"I'll come as far as the shops, then I must go home and make up a bed for you, Noddy," said Tessie. "It *will* be nice to have you staying for the night. Let Bumpy come with you in your car, and then you can bring him back here when you put your car away for the night."

So away went Noddy, Tessie and Bumpy in the

 car. Bumpy sat at the back, poking his head between them, enjoying himself.

Noddy set Tessie down at the shops, and then began to

look out for passengers as usual. First of all he took Miss Fluffy Cat, then he took Sally Skittle, then Mr. Noah, then Mr. Toy Dog. But all of them said that Bumpy was a dreadful nuisance, sitting at the back.

"Licking my head all over!" complained Sally Skittle. "Why doesn't he take a job at the post-office and lick stamps all the time? *Must* you have him with you, Noddy?"

"Just for today," said Noddy, and helped Sally Skittle out of his car. Bumpy at once slid down into the seat beside Noddy. He felt very, very grand sitting there!

"I really don't know why I like such a tiresome dog," said Noddy. "No, *don't* wag your tail like that—there isn't room on the front seat. Sit on it, Bumpy, sit on it."

## 5. QUITE A LOT HAPPENS

THAT evening, after Noddy had finished his
day's work, he drove home, and put his car
into the garage. He locked the door, and went to
wash himself and make himself tidy to go to
Tessie's house.

The Bumpy-Dog watched him, with his tail
down. He knew the time had come when he had
to stay in Noddy's house alone and guard it.
"Woof," he said, in a small sad voice.

"I'll leave you some meat in a dish," said
Noddy, putting some down. "Oh BUMPY!
Don't gobble so. Good gracious, dog, you've
swallowed the whole lot already! You can't even
have tasted it. What a waste! Well, you won't
have anything else—except this bone."

Bumpy sprang at the bone in glee, and lay down

34

peacefully gnawing it, while Noddy got himself ready. Noddy patted him and hurried out of the door before Bumpy could rush out with him. "Woof," said Bumpy again, very sadly.

Noddy went off to Tessie Bear's and had a very pleasant evening indeed. Tessie had a fine supper for him and for her uncle and aunt, and after that they played snap.

Tessie's Uncle Bear won easily. Then he told Noddy about three relations of his, called The Three Bears, whose home had been visited by a naughty little girl.

"And she sat down in their chairs and broke one, and she tasted their porridge and ate some all up, and then she went to sleep on one of their beds," said Uncle Bear.

Noddy was shocked. What a badly-behaved little girl! Tessie yawned. She had heard her

35

uncle tell the story of The Three Bears a great many times.

"Go to bed," said Uncle Bear. "You're tired, both of you. Tessie, show Noddy his little bedroom."

It was fun to sleep in someone else's house. Noddy liked it. He was soon fast asleep. Tessie Bear woke him in the morning.

"Get up, Noddy!" she said. "There's news! There's been *another* robbery in the night—someone has picked all Mr. Golly's ripe plums. But NOBODY can say it's you playing a trick, because you were here. Did you hear it raining in the night?"

"No. I didn't hear anything at all," said Noddy, still sleepy. "Good gracious—fancy Mr. Golly's plums being stolen! Well, I'm glad I slept here, and not at home! Mr. Plod is sure to hurry round to my house and say the robber had a car that went parp-parp like mine again!"

36

Noddy went to fetch his car after breakfast, wondering how the Bumpy-Dog had got on in the night.

He had quite a shock when he arrived at House-For-One. Big-Ears was there—and Mr. Plod—and the Tubby Bears—and Mr. Golly!

"Whatever are you all here for?" asked Noddy, in surprise.

"My plums were stolen in the night!" said Mr. Golly, fiercely.  "And I heard a car drive up—and when it stopped it said 'parp-parp' just like yours!"

"Well, I stayed the night at Tessie Bear's house," said Noddy. "So there! Her uncle and aunt will tell you. And what was more, I didn't even have my car with me. I left it locked in the garage. So it WASN'T me, and it WASN'T my car!"

"Dear me—is that so?" said Mr. Plod, surprised. "Well, I must say I'm glad to hear that.

37

Of course if you were staying at Tessie Bear's house, you couldn't have taken Mr. Golly's plums."

"Anyway, it's not like our Noddy to *steal* things," said Big-Ears. "I thought he might have taken my washing for a bit of fun—but he

certainly wouldn't steal Mr. Big-Bear's flowers or Mr. Golly's plums."

"Wuff-wuff-wuff!" barked the Bumpy-Dog from inside Noddy's house. He flung himself against the door and it shook from top to bottom.

"Don't, Bumpy, don't! You'll break it down!" cried Noddy, and ran to unlock the door. Bumpy came out like a bullet from a gun and flung himself rapturously on everyone. They went down like skittles, even Big-Ears. Then Bumpy ran round licking everyone with joy, his tail thumping against them as he went.

"GO HOME TO TESSIE BEAR, YOU RUDE, ROUGH DOG!" commanded Mr. Plod, in such a fierce voice that even Big-Ears quaked in his shoes. Bumpy put his tail down and shot off at once. Everyone heaved sighs of relief.

"Well, I'll be going," said Mr. Plod. "Sorry to have been cross with you yesterday, Noddy. I only hope I catch the thief before he does any more damage. Coming, Mr. Golly and Mr. Big-Bear? We may as well go along together. What about you, Big-Ears?"

"I'll stay and have a talk with Noddy," said Big-Ears. "This is all very, very peculiar!"

Big-Ears was very nice to Noddy. He was really very sorry for saying that Noddy had taken his washing. Noddy went to open his garage to take out his car.

"I'll run you back to your house, Big-Ears," he said. "You haven't your bicycle with you."

He swung open the garage doors—and then stared in amazement. "Big-Ears—look—what's been happening to my *car*? It's covered with mud! It's DREADFULLY dirty! Oh, Big-Ears, what *can* have happened? It was quite clean when I left it here last night!"

## 6. NODDY HAS A WONDERFUL IDEA

BIG-EARS was most astonished to see such a dirty little car. It gave a tiny hoot as they looked at it. "Parp-parp."

"Why don't you hoot properly?" said Noddy, surprised, and went to look at the hooter. "Oh, Big-Ears, LOOK! Someone has tied string very tightly round and round the rubber hooter, so that it can't hoot properly!"

"Noddy! The thief comes here each night and takes *your* car!" cried Big-Ears. "He must have a key to your garage. He ties up the hooter each night so that it can't hoot loudly and give him away—but it just manages to hoot a small 'parp-parp' and that's what made everyone think it was *your* car—and that you must be driving it!"

"And it's all muddy because the thief took it out in the rain last night!" said Noddy. "And LOOK—here's a plum. That *shows* that someone took my car up to Mr. Golly's orchard last night. Big-Ears—who is it?"

Mrs. Tubby Bear came to speak to them from next door. "What's the matter?" she said. "I heard the Bumpy-Dog barking at the top of his voice in the middle of the night. He woke us all up."

"Oh dear—why ever didn't you ask Mr. Tubby Bear to find out why he barked?" said Big-Ears.

"Well, I thought Noddy was at home," said Mrs. Tubby Bear. "Do tell me what has happened."

So they told her, and she was most surprised. "Your poor car!" she said to Noddy. "It must have hated being taken away by someone else each night. How did the thief get a key to your garage, Noddy?"

"Well, I had two keys, and I lost one a week ago," said Noddy. "So I expect the thief found it. Big-Ears—how can we catch him? Do you think he'll come again tonight?"

"Yes, I expect so," said Big-Ears. "We shall have to watch for him. But it's no good watching inside your house, Noddy. We'd never be outside quickly enough to get him. We must watch from somewhere *out*side."

"But where?" said Noddy, looking up and down the road. "There's nowhere we can hide and yet watch my garage at the same time."

"No, there isn't," said Big-Ears, frowning. "It's a pity there isn't a post-box anywhere near. We could have hidden behind that."

43

"We could make one, Big-Ears!" said Noddy, his head nodding up and down excitedly. "I don't mean a big heavy one. But can't we get some big sheets of paper, and paint them red, and roll them up to look like post-boxes —*two*—one for me and one for you?"

"Yes—what a good idea! Yes, of course we could!" said Big-Ears. "And we'll paint your dustbin lid red to make a top to one post-box, and perhaps Mrs. Tubby Bear would lend us her dustbin lid too, for the second letter-box."

"And we'll make a slit, like all post-boxes have for posting letters in!" cried Noddy, dancing about in joy. "And we'll peep through those and keep watch. Oh, Big-Ears, what a WONDERFUL idea. Let's get some stiff paper and red paint and start straight away!"

Well, before the morning was ended, two very life-like post-boxes stood in Noddy's back-garden! They were made of stiff paper, painted scarlet,

44

NODDY AND BIG-EARS STARTED STRAIGHT AWAY TO
MAKE TWO POST-BOXES

with red-painted dustbin lids for tops—and each had a nice wide slit, which looked as if it was meant for letters to slip into—but which was really for Noddy and Big-Ears to peep through!

"Shall we borrow Bumpy-Dog and let him sleep in the car tonight?" said Noddy, his head nodding again. "That will stop the thief taking the car and driving it away before we can stop him. I don't want to lose my car, you know!"

"You are full of good ideas, Noddy," said Big-Ears, pleased. "Yes, we'll fetch him tonight. I'll get him if you like. We're going to have some *fun*, Noddy!"

## 7. WHEN THE MOON SHONE OUT

NODDY cleaned up his car in the afternoon and then went out to see if he could find any passengers. Big-Ears went shopping and bought some cakes for tea, and a jam sandwich, and a box of chocolates. He wanted to make a fuss of Noddy because he hadn't been very kind to him a day or two before.

They had a lovely tea together, and then Big-Ears played cards with Noddy until it got dark. "As soon as it is *really* dark we will take out our pretend letter-boxes," said Big-Ears. "The moon will be up later on, and we shall easily be able to keep a watch on your garage. I think I'd better slip up to Tessie Bear's now and fetch Bumpy."

So Big-Ears fetched Bumpy, and he was most surprised and pleased to see Noddy again. He rushed at him in joy, but Noddy skipped behind a chair.

"No, Bumpy! I am *not* going to be bumped over any more today. Lie down! Be quiet! Keep still! Good gracious, don't you understand *any* of those orders? Sit still and I'll sing you a song about yourself. I said SIT STILL!"

So Bumpy sat still, pricked up his ears and listened while Noddy sang to him.

> "He barks and he jumps,
> His tail wags and thumps,
> He leaps in the air like a frog!
> He barks and he runs,
> He gobbles up buns,
> This bumpity, thumpity, jumpity,
> terrible DOG!"

Big-Ears laughed, and Bumpy gave a delighted bark and flung himself on Noddy. But Noddy was still behind the chair. "No!" he said. "If you knock me over I'll *never* sing your song again. Never. Behave yourself!"

Soon Big-Ears saw that it was really dark. "Time to take out our post-boxes, Noddy," he said, so out they went with them, secretly and quietly. Noddy set his down across the road, and Big-Ears set his not far from Noddy's house. They each got inside their own, putting them over their heads and sliding them down carefully over their bodies. Ah—now they could easily peer through the slits at the top, just under the red-painted dustbin-lids.

Noddy's head was nodding so fast with excitement that his bell kept ringing, and he had to stop nodding. It would never do to give a warning to the thief!

The moon came up, and soon it was quite light. Noddy and Big-Ears could easily see Noddy's garage. Inside, curled up in the car, was the Bumpy-

Dog, very quiet and still. He had been told exactly what to do.

Nothing happened for a long, long time. Then Noddy heard footsteps, and his head began to nod again. His bell rang, and he heard a loud "SHHHHHSH!" from the post-box across the road. Even Big-Ears could hear his bell!

The footsteps came nearer and passed by Big-Ears' post-box. He peered out of the slit. Ah—it was only old Mr. Jumbo taking an evening stroll.

Then they heard more footsteps—who was it this time? Noddy peered out of his slit—goodness, it was Mr. Plod! There he was, pacing slowly by. And just as he passed by Noddy's box, Noddy sneezed.

"A-whooshhhoo!"

Mr. Plod was very startled indeed. He looked all round but he couldn't see anyone at all. Who had sneezed? It had sounded so very, very close. He looked at the red post-box. No—post-boxes didn't sneeze. Still—how very extraordinary!

MR. PLOD WAS VERY STARTLED. HE LOOKED ALL ROUND
BUT HE COULDN'T SEE ANYONE AT ALL

He went on his way, much to Noddy's relief. Noddy had really been rather afraid that Mr. Plod would lean against his post-box—then it would certainly have gone over!

Time went on. The moon climbed a little higher and then went behind a thick cloud. Now was the time for a thief to come—while it was so dark.

Big-Ears thought he heard something. Yes— someone had passed by his post-box like a shadow! Then Noddy's sharp ears heard the sound of a little click—someone was unlocking his garage doors! There wasn't a sound from the Bumpy-Dog—he had been told not to bark until he saw the thief.

Then everything happened at once. Oh, WHAT an excitement! Noddy's head began to nod again, and his bell jingled out loudly. "Stop thief, stop thief!" Wuff-wuff-WUFF! Jingle, jingle! "Hey, there, stop! WHO ARE YOU?"

## 8. OH, HOW *VERY* EXCITING!

THE thief had crept into the garage. He had got into the driving-seat. And then the Bumpy-Dog had leapt at him, and barked at the top of his voice!

In a terrible fright the thief sprang out of the car and rushed to the garage door. He managed to shut it on Bumpy's nose and then tore off down the street.

"After him!" yelled Big-Ears. The thief turned round at the shout and in great alarm saw two red post-boxes bobbing down the road after him.

Two post-boxes—with feet underneath! He was so frightened that he didn't even look where he was going. He fled round the corner, and bumped full tilt into Mr. Plod, who was just coming back. CRASH! They both fell over backwards. Mr. Plod sat up angrily.

"Now then—what... good gracious! Am I going mad—or can I see two post-boxes running about? I'm dreaming! And who's this fellow who knocked me over? Hey, you, come back!"

Mr. Plod ran after the thief, and the post-boxes ran after them both. Mr. Plod was dreadfully scared of them, and the thief was just as scared of Mr. Plod. Mr. Tubby Bear, coming back from a party, couldn't think *what* was happening. He scurried home at top speed when the two post-boxes went by. No wonder letters often got lost in the post, if *that* was the kind of thing post-boxes did at night!

The thief was gaining on everyone. Mr. Plod was too fat to run fast, and Noddy and Big-Ears found the post-boxes were difficult to run in. "Oh dear!" panted Noddy. "We can't catch him!"

But just then something shot past him like a rocket, barking excitedly. It was the Bumpy-

MR. PLOD RAN AFTER THE THIEF, AND THE POST-BOXES
RAN AFTER THEM BOTH

55

Dog! He had managed to squeeze his nose into the crack of the garage door, and swing it open. WUFF-WUFF-WUFF! What a chase!

Well, Bumpy caught the thief just as he had got to the river. There was a little boat there, all ready for the robber to sail away in. It was still half full of the plums he had piled there last night!

Bumpy leapt at him and down he went. Then Bumpy sat firmly on top of him, his tail going thump-thump-thump with joy. Up came Mr. Plod, panting. And some way behind came the red letter-boxes, their feet running fast beneath them.

"Keep that thief safe for me, Bumpy-Dog,"

ordered Mr. Plod, "while I find out what these post-boxes are doing. What peculiar goings-on! Now then, you two post-boxes, what's the meaning of this?"

Big-Ears wriggled out of his post-box, and then Noddy slid out of his. Mr. Plod stared in amazement. "What! You and Noddy! Big-Ears, what do you think you're doing?"

"The same as you—chasing that thief!" said Big-Ears, cheerfully. "Who is he? My word— it's Sammy Sailor-Doll! Well, who would have thought it! Shame on you, Sammy—taking Noddy's car and going out robbing people at night! Get off him, Bumpy-Dog. Mr. Plod's going to lock him up."

"Oh no, oh no!" said Sammy Sailor-Doll, and he knelt down in front of Mr. Plod.

"Oh yes, oh yes," said Mr. Plod. "Get up! Pretending you're sorry like that! Big-Ears, let's

put him inside one of your peculiar post-boxes
—he can't possibly try to run away if he's in one
of those. It will be an easy way of taking him to
the police-station!"

So off they went with the sailor doll inside
a red post-box, the dustbin lid still on top. He

didn't like it at
all—and he didn't
like the Bumpy-Dog
sniffing around his
ankles either!

On the way they
passed Tessie Bear's
house. "Oh—let's
take Bumpy back
to her—and tell
her all that's
happened," said
Noddy. "Look—
they're still up,
there's a light on!"

"All right—we'll do that," said Big-Ears, who
was longing to tell someone all their exciting
news. "We'll take the other post-box with us
and show Tessie's uncle how we hid inside it.
Come on, Bumpy—and do stop thumping your

tail round my legs. I know you're pleased with yourself—but you very nearly didn't get out of Noddy's garage, you know!"

And now Noddy, Big-Ears and the Bumpy-Dog are all in Tessie Bear's house, drinking hot cocoa and eating chocolate biscuits, and telling their exciting tale.

"Oh, I *wish* I'd been there!" says little Tessie Bear, looking perfectly sweet in her dressing-gown. "Oh, I'm *glad* the thief has been caught. Oh, how I'd have liked to see you rushing along in the post-boxes!"

"WUFF WUFF!" says the Bumpy-Dog, putting a big paw on Tessie's knee.

"No, you can't have any more chocolate biscuits," says Tessie. "You've had five already. No, you can't have a bun either."

"He doesn't want a bun or a biscuit!" says Noddy. "He wants to sing you his Special Song. Listen, Tessie! This is the song of the Bumpy-Dog.

He barks and he jumps,
His tail wags and thumps,
He leaps in the air like a frog!
He barks and he runs,
He gobbles up buns,
This bumpity, thumpity, jumpity,
    terrible DOG!

Now altogether:
    This bumpity, thumpity, jumpity,
    terrible DOG!"

Everyone yelled the last line at the tops of their voices, and the Bumpy-Dog leapt at Noddy in delight. You can guess what Noddy said, I expect.

"Oh, DON'T, Bumpy-Dog! DON'T!"